STAR JUMPER

Kids Can Press acknowledges the financial support of the Government of Ontario,
through the Ontario Media Development Corporation's Ontario Book Initiative,
and the Government of Canada, through the BPIDP, for our publishing activity.

Published in Canada by   Published in the U.S. by
Kids Can Press Ltd.   Kids Can Press Ltd.
25 Dockside Drive   2250 Military Road
Toronto, ON M5A 0B5   Tonawanda, NY 14150

www.kidscanpress.com

Edited by Tara Walker
Designed by Karen Powers

Manufactured in Altona, Manitoba, Canada, in 5/2010 by Friesens Corporation

CM 06 0 9 8 7 6 5 4 3 2
CM PA 06 0 9 8 7 6 5

Library and Archives Canada Cataloguing in Publication

Asch, Frank
    Star jumper : Journal of a cardboard genius / Frank Asch.

ISBN 978-1-55337-886-0 (bound)
ISBN 978-1-55337-887-7 (pbk.)

I. Title.
PZ7.A778St 2006   j813'.54   C2005-903654-0

Kids Can Press is a ℓ☺ⓝ𝗌™ Entertainment company

STAR JUMPER

JOURNAL OF A CARDBOARD GENIUS

by Frank Asch

Kids Can Press

To my big brother, John, who built me a telegraph for show and tell

Table of Contents

CHAPTER 1

My Mission

I found this notebook in the stationery aisle at
Food King. I don't know how much it cost because
my mom paid for it. But when I'm famous,
I predict it will sell for millions of dollars. Maybe
billions. It will be a historic document, like the
Magna Carta or the very first Superman comic.
Someday everyone is going to want to know what's
written here.

After paying for the groceries, Mom asked
the produce manager if she could have some
cardboard boxes.

"They're for my son," she said.

"We usually crush all our boxes, but you're in
luck," replied the manager. "A delivery just came in.
How many do you need?"

"According to my calculations, I'll need about ten boxes to build a decent-sized spaceship," I told him.

He smiled and took us to a room with enough cardboard boxes to build a fleet of star cruisers.

On the way home, I sat in the back of our van with the boxes and made some quick pencil sketches. By the time we pulled into our driveway, I knew exactly how I was going to use 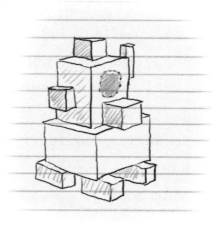 each box to construct the hull of my ship. That's the kind of genius I am. Not just brilliant, but fast!

I'd like to say I'm on a secret mission to save the world or something noble like that. But I'm not.

I just want to put a few light-years between me and my little brother. His name is Jonathan and he's evil. Seriously.

To be honest, some people actually like my little brother. Grown-ups are the ones most likely to suffer from this form of brain damage. "Oh, he's such a sweet child," they say. *Sweet?* They wouldn't say that if they had to live with him like I do.

First of all, Jonathan never shuts up. Talk. Talk. Talk! His mouth is like a hole in his brain where questions leak out. He even asks them in his sleep. I'm not kidding. He does it all the time. When he was

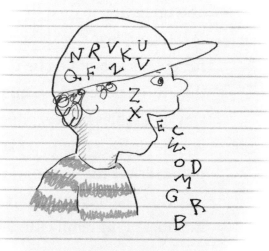

little, he asked questions like "Does mud have a belly button?" and "How come babies are born naked?" Now he wants to know things like "Who invented ice cream?" and "How come the moon is yellow?" Just try listening to babble like *that* all day long!

And what a klutz! If you don't believe me, just take Jonathan fishing and watch him try to put a worm on a hook. He can't do it! He tries, but he can't. The worm keeps falling on the ground, and I end up having to do it for him.

Okay. Maybe he's not evil. Maybe he's just rotten. But everything he does gets on my nerves: the way he never stops squirming when he sits, the way he shuffles his feet when he walks. Even the way he sleeps, curled up like a dog drooling on his pillow, drives me up the wall!

How that crybaby, brat, tattletale got to be a member of *my* family I'll never know. He sure doesn't have any of my good qualities. He knows nothing about dinosaurs or Z-Men or video games. He doesn't even know how to open a bottle of ketchup without getting it all over himself.

My mom says I'm normal. *Normal?* How can that be? She says all big brothers feel the way I do. But I know that's not true. There's a kid at school, Billy Rosenberg, who claims to actually *like* his little brother!

Mom tells me not to worry. She says, "It's just sibling rivalry, Alex." As if that explained it all. As if giving it a fancy name made it okay. According to her it's just a "phase" I'm going through.

Dad says, "You got all the love before your little brother came along. Now you're learning how to share it." I guess that's what you get when both your parents are psychiatrists: a lot of dumb advice. But it's not a phase I'm going through. *And I won't grow out of it!*

That's why I have to leave.

Any planet with a breathable atmosphere will do. Mountains and lakes and green grass and trees would be nice, too. And volcanoes. I really love volcanoes. The important thing is to get as far away from Jonathan and Planet Earth as possible. So far away that no one — not even NASA — will ever find me and bring me home.

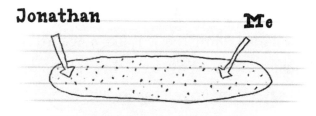

CHAPTER 2

My Spaceship

It's never easy doing anything when Jonathan is around. As soon as I brought the boxes inside the house, he latched on to me like a tick and started tugging on the belt loops of my jeans.

"Are you building something for me?" He pestered me all the way upstairs to my room.

One time I built Jonathan a simple telescope for show and tell. (I made it in five minutes from a piece of plastic I found in the trash, a broken magnifying glass, a paper towel roll and a little duct tape.) So now the creep expects me to devote my entire life to making things for him.

"Yeah, I'm building you a coffin," I said.

"I don't think so," he replied with that wormy little voice of his. "I think you're building me a castle. You're building me a castle so I can be a knight. Are you going to be my horse?"

"No," I said. "I'm *not* going to be your horse."

"That's okay. I'll be the king and you can be my servant."

"It's not a castle," I told him. "Now please go away!"

Mom once advised me, "Always say 'please' when talking to Jonathan. You'd be surprised at how effective it is." Well, so far it hasn't worked at all.

"I just want to watch," said Jonathan. He picked up the utility knife I was going to use to cut the cardboard. "And I want to help, too!"

"Give me that!" I grabbed the knife from his hand. "You're not supposed to play with knives. Now get out of here!"

"I get it," he said as I pushed him toward the door. "You want to surprise me. That's why you want me to leave."

"I want to surprise you all right," I said. And I thought to myself, *Won't you be surprised when you wake up some day and I'm gone. Gone forever and living on the other side of the galaxy!*

I shoved Jonathan into the hall and slammed the door in his face. You'd think he would catch my drift and go find something else to do. But he never does.

"I'll just guard the door so nobody bothers you!" he shouted.

"Thanks," I said and started to work.

I love cardboard. It's the perfect material for my kind of work. It's fast. It's flexible. It's everywhere. And it's free.

I began by installing the main power unit and Stellar Drive in the biggest box. This is also where I'll sleep and store food, water and spare cargo. The second biggest box is for the bridge of my ship, where the control panels and navigation equipment will be located. I'll be doing all my navigating electronically, but I cut a circular hole in this box so I can look out at the Milky Way anytime I want to.

In the third box I installed the master computer and radar dish. I built everything according to my own unique design, mostly with stuff I collect from the street on garbage day and keep in plastic bins under my bed. For example, my radar dish is made from:

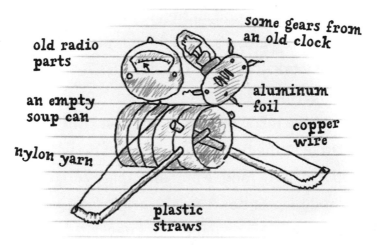

old radio parts

some gears from an old clock

an empty soup can

aluminum foil

copper wire

nylon yarn

plastic straws

Radar Dish

For homeland security reasons, I'm leaving out certain important details in this notebook. I wouldn't want my plans to fall into the wrong hands. But for those of you reading these notes hoping to build your own spaceship, I will give you one piece of free advice: always use duct tape, the silver kind. Never use Scotch tape or even masking tape. That stuff is so flimsy your ship will fall apart before you reach the Van Allen belts.

Of course I didn't make everything all at once. I've been planning and working on the main components of my spaceship for weeks. As soon as I finished something, I put it on the top shelf of my closet, where Jonathan can't reach.

The hardest part to construct was the Stellar Drive. It doesn't work like most of today's spaceships. I'd be an old man with a long gray beard before I left the solar system in a spacecraft of that sort. My engine works according to my very own space-warp design, which I based on the latest developments in superstring theory. Instead of propelling you through space like a bullet, my Stellar Drive shrinks the space between where you are and where you want to go. When you can shrink a trillion miles down to a trillionth of an inch, you can go anywhere in the universe in the blink of an eye. Best of all, my Stellar Drive requires such a small amount of energy it runs on only two AA batteries!

It took me less than an hour and a half to build the hull and outfit my spaceship. That's probably a record of some sort. I could have done it sooner, but Jonathan wouldn't stop bugging me.

He kept peering through the keyhole and saying things like "Hey, I can't see anything. Get out of the way!"

It got so annoying that I had to tape over the keyhole. But that didn't shut him up. "Don't forget to put a flag on top!" he said. "And make sure the walls are strong! That's the whole idea of a castle. The walls have to be strong and tall. The taller, the better ..."

After a while he started shoving crayon drawings under my door.

"You see? That's what it has to look like. Make sure it looks *exactly* like this!" he shouted as each new drawing came sliding toward me. "See the turrets? It's got to have lots of turrets."

Because he couldn't see what was happening, every second sentence out of his mouth was "So how's it going?" and "Are you done yet?"

I just ignored him, which is the one thing he really hates. Before long he began pounding on my door.

"Hey, let me in!" he shouted. "I want to take a nap!"

Take a nap? Give me a break! Since when does a six year old *want* to take a nap?

"Take a nap in your own room," I told him.

"I can't. My bed is too lumpy," he whined and kept on pounding.

The noise was really loud but I just tuned it out. My ship was ready to test.

I stepped back to admire my handiwork. What a beauty! Every part of it was unique. Every part of it was *me*. If everything worked according to plan, I'd soon be free of Jonathan forever!

I climbed aboard and flipped on the main power unit. Then I turned up the throttle just one notch. Suddenly my spaceship leaped into the air and hovered a few inches from the ceiling.

Wow! This ship is as jumpy as a frog! I thought. And right then and there I named her:

CHAPTER 3

My Spacesuit

I cut the power and Star Jumper settled back to the floor.

"From now on, it's just you and me, Star Jumper," I said out loud. "We're going places! New worlds are calling to us and the universe is the limit!"

I was so excited that my hands were shaking. *Calm down*, I told myself. *You're not ready yet. Not by a long shot. For one thing, you still need to make yourself a spacesuit.*

I didn't have the right stuff in my plastic bins or closet to make a good spacesuit. But I was pretty sure I'd find everything I needed in our attic.

When I opened my bedroom door, Jonathan was standing there with a big squinty-eyed grin on his face.

"So how's my castle?" he asked. "Is it ready yet?"

One look at Star Jumper and his big grin turned into a big pout.

"Hey, wait a minute! Where's my castle?"

"I never said I'd build you a castle," I told him.

"Yes, you did," he insisted. "A castle with turrets. And a moat and a drawbridge and you were going to be my horse and bring me breakfast in bed!"

Did I mention that my brother is delusional?

"Horses don't serve breakfast in bed," I snapped and shoved him out of the way.

"They do if you're the king! Kings get anything they want whenever they want it. They can take baths in whipped cream if they want to!"

He was walking so close behind me it made my skin creep. Remember how Peter Pan lost his shadow and Wendy sewed it on for him? Well, it's like that, only the opposite, with my little brother: Jonathan wants to get rid of my shadow so he can take its place!

When I reached the pull-down steps in the hall, I told him, "Look, I'm going upstairs to the attic now and you're afraid of all the spiders and cobwebs and *vampire* bats that live up there, so why don't you do yourself a favor and go outside and play in traffic or something?"

Jonathan tried to look tough, but I could tell I had scared him. He hates bats. Even fake Halloween bats.

"Who says there are bats in the attic?"

"No one has to say it," I told him. "It's a fact."

Of course, I was making this all up. I just wanted to get rid of him. I could tell it was working because the blood was starting to drain from his face.

"Well, I don't care about spiders or cobwebs or *bats*. They don't scare me one bat — er … I mean bit!" said Jonathan. But he didn't follow me into the attic. He just sat on the rug in the hall and waited for me to come down.

The attic has got to be my most favorite place in our house. Both my parents are pack rats. They never throw anything away. It all goes up into the attic with stuff from my grandparents and yard sales and things that got left behind by the last owners of the house. It's like a museum up there. A museum of odds and ends, dusty old stuff from long ago and just plain junk.

Pack Rats

Mom

Dad

It only took me a few minutes to find everything I needed:

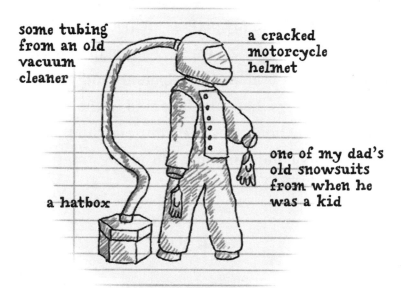

some tubing from an old vacuum cleaner

a cracked motorcycle helmet

one of my dad's old snowsuits from when he was a kid

a hatbox

Spacesuit Design

It's amazing what you can build from common household items. I'm surprised nobody else seems to know this. It must be one of the best-kept secrets in the world.

When I climbed down from the attic, Jonathan was busy at work on a new set of crayon drawings.

"It won't be hard to make that dumb spaceship into a cool castle," he said, poking his crayon at the paper. "See, all you have to do is make a few changes ..."

I tried to get to my room before he could sneak in. But carrying all that stuff slowed me down. As I closed my bedroom door, I saw Jonathan's foot disappear under my bed. Once he's under there, it's impossible to pry him out. Even poking at him with a hockey stick doesn't work.

I thought about complaining to my mom. But I knew that would only create a big scene. In the end I'd still have to listen to him shout and pound on my door. Sometimes when stuff like this happens, I lose it, have a tantrum and start throwing things. But not today. *Just be cool*, I told myself. *Let the worm spy on you all he wants. At least that way he'll be quiet.*

So I pretended Jonathan wasn't under my bed and started constructing my Oxygen Generator.

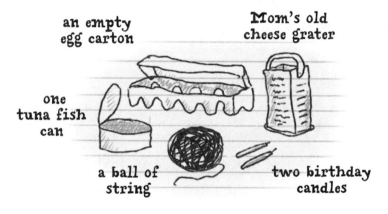

an empty
egg carton

Mom's old
cheese grater

one
tuna fish
can

a ball of
string

two birthday
candles

Materials for Oxygen Generator

It took about twenty-five minutes to build and install the Oxygen Generator in the hatbox. After a quick test, I inserted the vacuum cleaner hose in the hatbox lid. Then I ran the other end of the hose to the motorcycle helmet and sealed everything with duct tape.

I was moving right along until I ran out of tape. *No big deal,* I thought. *There's another roll in the junk drawer in the kitchen. It will only take me a minute to run downstairs to get it.*

I was so involved in my work that I totally forgot about Jonathan until I ran into Mom in the kitchen, making dinner.

"Have you seen your little brother?" she asked. "I haven't heard a peep out of him for quite a while."

"He's in *my* room," I said as I found the tape and closed the drawer.

"Oh, that's nice." She smiled. "I'm glad you two are playing quietly for a change. Don't go far. Dinner will be ready soon."

Playing with Jonathan? Sometimes I wonder if my mom knows me at all.

I had only been gone a few minutes but I was starting to worry. I ran upstairs, taking three steps at a time. When I opened my bedroom door, my worst fear was staring me in the face.

Jonathan was no longer under my bed. He was inside Star Jumper. His hands were on the controls and he was grinning like a maniac.

"Hey, this thing works great!" he cried as Star Jumper lifted off the floor and drifted toward the ceiling.

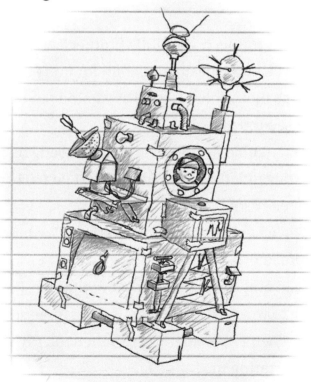

CHAPTER 4

The Problem

"You little creep!" I jumped onto my bed and reached into Star Jumper. I flipped the main power unit off, guided the ship back to the floor and yanked Jonathan out.

"All I did was push one button and — WOW!"

"You're lucky you didn't push the one that says 'Mega-Jump' or you'd be lost in space by now," I said and shoved him toward the door.

"You're just saying that, right?"

"Try it and see," I told him. "Now get out of here! I've got important things to do."

"No way!" he yelled, crossing his arms over his chest. "If you throw me out, I'll tell Mom what you're up to."

That's just like Jonathan. The first word out of

his mouth when he was a baby was "Mom." But that was only because he was getting ready to use it in the sentence "I'll *tell* Mom …"

Actually, Jonathan was a cute baby. I even liked him a little back then. He had a way of smiling at you that was sort of nice. Then he started to walk and talk and stick to me like a fresh coat of paint. It didn't take long before that cute little smile made me want to puke.

"You tell Mom what I'm doing and I'll stick you in that spaceship and send you to Pluto!" I threatened.

"Pluto, the dog at Disney World?" he replied cheerfully.

"No, Pinhead! Pluto the planet!"

"I think I might like that," he said.

"No, you wouldn't," I told him. "Pluto is the farthest planet from the sun. You'd freeze to death in an instant."

"Doesn't matter. If I tell Mom, she'll take it away from you. Kids aren't supposed to have *real* spaceships. Even pinheads know that!"

He's a smart little brat. I'll give him that much.

"Okay, you can stay in my room. But keep your mouth shut. And don't touch anything."

"Deal," he said.

"In fact, you have to stay on my bed. Got it?"

"Got it," he answered, jumping headfirst into my pillows.

"You better," I said. "If your toes so much as touch the floor, I'm going to send you across the galaxy into a black hole!"

For once Jonathan kept his word. He was perfectly still and quiet, watching my every move.

Just as I finished my spacesuit, Mom called us

down for dinner. It was my favorite, spaghetti and meatballs, but I had to eat with my eyes closed. That may sound strange, but you'd want to close your eyes, too, if you had to sit across from my brother at the dinner table. I know it's hard to believe, but Mom and Dad still let him eat with his hands! It's *so* disgusting to watch. If I don't shut my eyes, I might throw up.

Jonathan picks up the spaghetti like a handful of worms as he looks for the longest strand on his plate. Then he sucks it through his puckered lips with a slurping sound, splattering spaghetti sauce all over his cheeks and nose. Sometimes he even manages to get sauce on his forehead.

It's almost impossible to watch without gagging. But Mom and Dad don't seem to mind. When I complain, they just say things like "Kids grow up too fast nowadays. Let him have his childhood." *Childhood?* My little brother eats like a wild animal!

I had hoped Jonathan would keep to our bargain. But of course, he didn't. As Mom brought out dessert, he said, "You should see what Alex is making in his room."

I gave him a dirty look and kicked him under the table. Hard. I know it had to hurt. But the creep just smiled while spaghetti sauce dripped like vampire blood down his chin. He didn't even wince. Jonathan's incredible that way. When he doesn't want to show pain, he can withstand a bazooka blast without flinching. But when he wants to get you in trouble, watch out. Then all you have to do is nudge his elbow by mistake and he'll turn on the tears and make enough noise to knock plates off the shelf.

"You have a very talented older brother," said Dad. "What is it you're making this time, Alex?"

"Well … er …"

"It's a castle," said Jonathan. "And it's just for me."

"Isn't that sweet," said my mom, plopping some peach cobbler in front of me. "I'm glad to know you two are finally expressing the positive side of your relationship. I'll have to come up and see the castle after your dad and I finish with the dishes."

"No," said Jonathan. "It's a surprise. You can't see it until it's finished."

"That's right," I added. "You can't see it until it's finished."

After dinner Jonathan tried to get back in my room. But I barred the doorway.

"You're banished!"

"What for?" he asked. "I didn't tell."

"For being a monster," I said. "Besides, I'm not done expressing the *negative side* of our relationship."

Just then Dad called Jonathan to watch his favorite TV show, *Thursday Night Wrestling*, and he scooted downstairs. What a relief!

I locked my bedroom door and got to work solving my next major problem: how to get Star Jumper, which is much too big to fit through a window or door, out of my bedroom. My original plan was to wait till everyone was asleep, and then carry her piece by piece into the backyard. With a little luck, I'd have just enough time to put her back together and blast off before anyone realized what I was up to.

I guess it was an okay plan, but I was starting to worry about going up and down stairs in the middle of the night. What would I do if someone woke up?

If only I could take off on my journey into outer space from *inside* my bedroom. *What a crazy idea,* I thought. Then my eyes wandered over to my desk and I saw Einstein.

CHAPTER 5

The Atom Slider

I used to have tropical fish, but Jonathan killed them all. It had to be him. Mom or Dad wouldn't do something mean like that. He probably did it to get back at me for something I did to him. Or something he imagined I did to him. Who knows what goes on in that evil brain of his? This much I'm sure of: one day when I was at school and Jonathan was sick at home, someone turned up the heater in my tropical fish tank. When I came back, my fish were boiled — each and every one of them! Of course, the creep turned down the thermostat so I couldn't prove a thing. Clever. Diabolical. Jonathan in a nutshell!

I used to have Angelfish, Red Scissortails, Firemouths, New Guinea Tigerfish and Dwarf

Puffers. Now all I have is one goldfish, Einstein, who I keep in a small bowl on my desk.

There's a big piece of pink coral plopped right in the middle of Einstein's bowl. The only way he can get from one side of the bowl to the other is to swim through one of its openings. As I watched him lazily thread his way through the holes in the coral, I suddenly had such a stupendously brilliant idea I hollered, "*Eureka!*"

"Eureka" is what Archimedes is supposed to have cried when he discovered how to measure the density of gold. The story goes that the old Greek scientist was taking a bath at the time. He got so excited when the solution came to him that he jumped out of the tub and ran naked through the streets of Greece crying, "Eureka! Eureka! I found it! I found it!"

Well, I didn't go running through the house naked or anything like that, but my shout must have been pretty loud because Mom called out from her office, "Is everything all right, Alex?"

"Yeah, I'm fine, Mom! Really fine!" I hollered back.

Boy! Was I pumped! The solution was so ingenious. I'll try to explain it as simply as I can. The walls of my bedroom appear to be solid. But appearances can be deceiving. (The longer I study science, the more I realize that hardly anything is the way it seems. Take my brother, for example.

Jonathan   Jonathan

As he appears   As he really is

He seems like a normal kid. But in reality he's an abomination. A fiend. A two-legged plague!) The walls of my bedroom are actually made of atoms, and science tells us there are spaces between individual atoms. Not just spaces, but big spaces. Enormous spaces.

V A S T   S P A C E S !

See what I'm getting at?

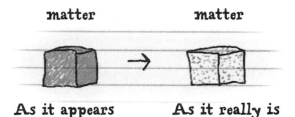

matter   matter

As it appears   As it really is

Einstein doesn't have to bore his way through the coral to get to the other side of his tank. All he has to do is swim through one of the holes. As long as he doesn't bump into the coral, there's no problem. Likewise, all I have to do is figure out a way to keep Star Jumper's atoms from bumping into the atoms of my house. Then Star Jumper will pass right through its walls just like Einstein passes through the pink coral!

What could be simpler? I don't know why everyone makes such a big deal about being a genius. For me it's easy.

Once I had my insight, the rest was a piece of cake. The math took about twenty minutes. Then I sketched out the basic design. I called my new invention an Atom Slider because it allows one atom to slide past another without touching.

Luckily, I found everything I needed to build my new invention in the bins under my bed:

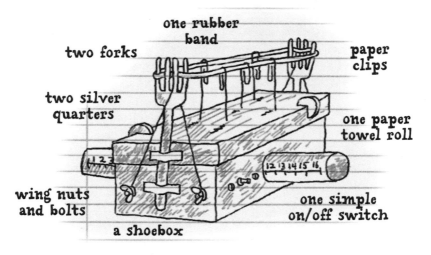

one rubber band

two forks

paper clips

two silver quarters

one paper towel roll

wing nuts and bolts

one simple on/off switch

a shoebox

The Atom Slider

I finished my Atom Slider in less than an hour. Another record for the history books. That made two in just one day! Even Einstein, the *real* Einstein, wasn't that brilliant!

But it was getting late. Pretty soon it would be bedtime. I quickly installed the Atom Slider in Star

Jumper's control panel. Then I gathered some supplies for the trip:

- √ a change of clothes
- √ my toothbrush
- √ snacks (seven granola bars, three banana nut cupcakes, one large bag of potato chips and two boxes of pretzels)
- √ a first aid kit
- √ my Warrior cards
- √ all my Z-Men comic books
- √ my notebooks (this one and the one where I write down all my scientific formulas)

As I was stowing away the last few items in Star Jumper's cargo hold, I sensed Jonathan, like an evil force, lurking outside my bedroom door.

"What do you want?" I yelled.

"Can I come in?"

"No. Go away!"

"You missed a great wrestling match. Want to hear about it?"

"No."

"Aww … come on. Open the door. I want to see how my castle is coming along."

"No."

"So you admit it. You *are* working on my castle."

"No."

"Aren't you going to say anything but no?"

"No!"

There was a long silence. Then I heard Dad's footsteps in the hall.

"What are you doing still awake?" he said and I heard him snatch up Jonathan in his arms. "You're supposed to be in bed by now."

"Alex is up," said Jonathan.

Dad must have tickled Jonathan just then because I heard him giggle.

"Alex! It's past your bedtime, too," Dad called

through the door. "Tomorrow is a school day."

"Okay, Dad," I called back.

I covered Star Jumper with a sheet, put on my pajamas and climbed into bed.

Actually, Dad, tomorrow isn't a school day. Not for me at least! I said to myself as I lay on my back in the dark. *In fact, unless I start one myself on my new planet, I'm never going to school again.*

My new planet. Those words sounded so sweet. I let them melt on my tongue like a cool lick of ice cream on a hot summer day.

But I didn't let myself fall asleep.

After a while, Mom came in to say good night. She always does that, even if she's really busy.

When I was younger she used to read to me almost every night. Dad, too. Now I'm bigger, so they read mostly to Jonathan. Sometimes I listen in. But when you're my age, you don't want to hear the same stories that your six-year-old brother likes. Especially when they used to be your favorite stories and now they're his.

As soon as Mom came in, she went right over to Star Jumper.

"It's so nice that you're building something for Jonathan. Can I take a peek?" she said and took hold of the sheet.

I sat bolt upright in bed.

"No, don't!" I snapped. "You'll … you'll spoil the surprise."

"Well, I wouldn't want to do that." She let go of the sheet and I breathed a sigh of relief. "But I am so proud of you, dear. So very proud."

Then Mom tucked me in and gave me a good-night kiss. It was just like every other good-night kiss she ever gave me, but tonight it *felt* different. *That's the last good-night kiss I'll ever get from my mom,* I thought.

Just as she was about to shut the door, I called out to her, "I'll never forget you, Mom!"

She stopped and gave me a funny look.

Then she smiled that nice smile of hers.

"And I'll never forget you either, Alex," she said and turned out the light.

For a while, I just lay there in the dark thinking *dark* thoughts. I hadn't even left yet and already I was missing Mom and Dad and my house and my school and my friends. Heck! I was missing everyone on the planet! Everyone that is, but Jonathan.

It's not fair, I thought. *After all, it's his fault, not mine, that I'm leaving. If it wasn't for that pain-in-the-butt brother of mine, I could live out my days on Earth basking forever in the glory of my genius and fame!*

I lay in my bed for what seemed like hours, waiting for everyone to fall asleep. Then, when the house was dead quiet, I got out of bed and turned on my desk lamp. It was 1:30 a.m. Takeoff time!

CHAPTER 6

Good-Bye, Earth

Only one last detail remained. I shoved a towel under my door so the light from my room wouldn't shine into the hall. Then I sat at my desk and wrote Mom and Dad a good-bye note:

Dear Mom and Dad,

By the time you read this, I'll be on the other side of the galaxy. But please don't be sad and don't try to follow me. You'd only be wasting your time because I'm light-years ahead of all the other rocket scientists on this planet.

I just want you to know Jonathan is the reason I'm leaving. Not YOU! I know he's not your fault. After all, you also had me and look how wonderful I turned out!

I feel a little guilty leaving you behind to deal with him. But he's your kid. Not mine. Good luck. You'll need it.

I love you both.

Your good son,

ALEX

P.S. Don't worry about me. I took my toothbrush and I promise to eat right whenever I can.

I left the note on my desk, where they'd be sure to find it in the morning. Then I put on my spacesuit, zipping it up airtight, and climbed into Star Jumper. At last my journey had begun! I gave Einstein a wink good-bye, switched on the Atom Slider and engaged the Stellar Drive.

Star Jumper slowly lifted off the floor. I checked my control panel. Green lights were flashing. Energy levels were positive. All systems were *Go.*

As Star Jumper neared the ceiling, my stomach began to tighten. I double-checked the

Atom Slider to make sure the settings were right. If my calculations were off by even half a decimal point, the ship would just bump against the ceiling.

But everything worked perfectly. (Yet another amazing scientific accomplishment to add to my ever-growing list!)

Star Jumper floated up through the ceiling and the attic like a balloon through a cloud. *Boy, I'm sure going to miss this attic,* I thought. *I could search the whole universe and never find another like it.*

Star Jumper carried me up through the roof into the starry night sky. I turned off the Atom Slider and let the ship drift with the breeze for a few moments. Below me I spied Jonathan through his bedroom window. I saw him clearly in the glow of his clown face night-light. He was fast asleep in his bed, curled up like a golden retriever.

"Good-bye, Fido!" I waved and slid the Stellar Drive into Phase 1 Jump Mode. In less than the blink of an eye, Star Jumper leaped thousands of miles. The view out my porthole instantly went blank. Then slowly my eyes adjusted and I saw the Milky Way. Star Jumper was hovering halfway between Earth and the moon!

If you think stars look beautiful from Earth, you should see them from outer space. They're like diamonds. The colors are so pure and bright. It was like floating in a bowl of star soup.

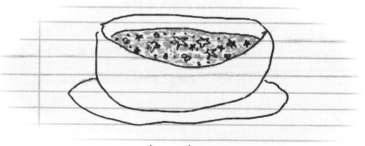

Star Soup

There's got to be a new home out there for me! I thought. *Good-bye, Earth! Hello, Universe!*

I was excited, but not too excited to properly test out my spacesuit before actually leaving the solar system. I tightened my helmet and checked for air leaks. Then I opened Star Jumper's hatch and went for a little space walk. Actually, I don't know why they call it space walking. There was nothing to walk on, not even air. It should be called space floating. I felt like a helium balloon and someone had just cut my string.

On my right was the moon, like a big yellow pumpkin, and below me was Earth. I could see its continents and oceans spread out like green and blue blankets covered with streaks of whipped-cream clouds. I could see America directly below me and Europe and Africa sliding into view. At that moment I couldn't think of myself as belonging to just one nation or continent. I was an Earthling — pure and simple. "Au revoir, my pretty planet!" I said and climbed back into Star Jumper.

At last, I was *really* ready. I set my course toward the center of the galaxy, where I figured there'd be the highest concentration of new planets to explore. I was just about to shift the Stellar Drive into Phase 7 Mega-Jump Mode when all of a sudden it hit me: *What if the planet I go to isn't friendly? What if it's inhabited by a race of highly intelligent sharks and I end up inside a seaweed sandwich? What if my new planet is still in its dinosaur phase and I travel halfway across*

the universe only to be squashed by an alien brontosaurus? Or fed, piece by piece, to a nest full of baby pterodactyls? Or what if my new neighbors are friendly but they think I'm a scout for an invasion from Earth? I could be zapped, grilled and pickled in a nanosecond!

I thought I had figured out everything. Crossed all my t's and dotted all my i's. Left nothing to chance. But, obviously, I hadn't. Space can be a dangerous place. Everybody knows that. What was I thinking? How could I leave Earth without some kind of self-defense? I can't believe how close I came to making a giant mistake. How dumb can a true genius be?

What Star Jumper needed was some kind of security system. A stun gun or blaster. Maybe even a death ray! I still had a chance to fix things. But that meant turning back and going home. Back to the plastic bins under my bed and all that good stuff in the attic.

What I thought was my final departure turned out to be nothing more than a practice run. *What a bummer!* I can't begin to tell you how disappointed I felt. On the other hand, my spaceship, spacesuit and Atom Slider had all performed perfectly. So what if I was temporarily going back home? I had a lot to be proud of already.

When a genius makes history, he has to expect some minor delays. I'm underlining that statement so scholars will know which of my many wise sayings I myself consider the most brilliant. I have no doubt that someday these words of mine will be quoted often and engraved on many a bronze plaque.

I took one last look at the Milky Way.

"Don't feel bad, Universe. I shall return!" I said and set a course back toward Earth. Back through the Van Allen belts, the stratosphere and the troposphere, back through the clouds, back to my town, my house and, finally, my bedroom.

CHAPTER 7

Mission Delayed

This morning I woke up in Star Jumper. I guess I must have fallen asleep at the controls before I had a chance to crawl into bed. My mouth tasted funny and my left foot was numb. The first sound I heard was Jonathan running up and down the hall having his first temper tantrum of the day.

"Where's my pencil box?" he demanded. "No! That's the old one. I want the new one. The *new* blue one!" Sometimes he treats Mom and Dad like hired help. As if he's Lord of the Manor and they're nothing more than his private servants.

I was itching to stay home from school and get started on Star Jumper's security system. But last month I faked tonsillitis three times in three weeks. Mom was starting to get a wee bit suspicious. So I got dressed and went downstairs for breakfast.

"How's my castle coming along?" asked the rat.

Jonathan looked all bright-eyed and shiny —
like he'd had a terrific night's sleep and was now
charged with fresh energy to make my life
miserable.

"Great," I lied. "Just great."

"How about some pancakes, boys?" asked
my mom.

Mom's pancakes aren't just good. They're
superior — light and fluffy, just the way I like
them. But I can't stand to eat pancakes when my
brother is around. The way he licks the syrup like
a cat makes my stomach turn.

"No thanks, Mom," I said and reached for a
box of cornflakes.

"No you don't!" Jonathan grabbed the box out
of my hand. "You ate Toasty Flakes yesterday! So
today it's my turn!" He shoved another box of
cereal in my face. "Today you eat Honey Puffs!"

"Jonathan, don't be rude!" snapped my mom.

"Never mind," I told her and snatched the Honey Puffs out of Jonathan's hand.

Why should I care? Soon I'll be eating exotic fruits for breakfast on some faraway planet with no little brothers in sight.

Exotic Fruit

After breakfast I put my special notebook in my backpack. I was going to school all right. But I wasn't going to be doing much schoolwork. Every chance I got, I planned to devote to my security system.

Jonathan and I both go to Whitman Elementary School. He's a first grader, so I don't see much of him during the day. But we ride the same bus. That wouldn't be so bad if I could sit far away from the little cretin. Maybe then I could pretend we were on different buses. But Dad insists we sit together.

The reason for this is a couple of second graders who don't like Jonathan. *Imagine that!* These pint-sized hooligans' favorite pastime is stealing my little brother's hat and throwing it all over the bus for the sheer pleasure of watching him have a conniption. Jonathan claims they're bullies, but I suspect he's getting exactly what he deserves.

Unfortunately, Dad doesn't see it that way.

"My big brother always protected me from bullies," he took me aside and told me one day. "That's what big brothers do." So I have to sit next to Jonathan on the bus. Personally, I'd rather get a tooth drilled. Nobody else sits next to *their* little brother. Not even Billy Rosenberg. It's humiliating. How does Dad know what big brothers do, anyway? Where is it written? Did he conduct a survey?

This morning all Jonathan wanted to do was talk about *Thursday Night Wrestling*. When I say talk about it, I mean TALK ABOUT IT! I swear he had the whole show memorized blow by blow.

"Look," I told him again and again, "I don't care how Bone Crusher threw his own teammate out of the ring. I hate wrestling!"

"Yeah, but you're going to love the next part!" he'd say, and ten minutes later he was still talking about it. I couldn't wait to get off the bus. Those seven hours of school away from my brother are the only time I get any peace.

I'd tell you about my school day but I don't remember much. I guess I paid enough attention to my teachers to get by. Maybe I even raised my hand and answered a few questions. I probably talked to some friends, too. But I couldn't say who.

What I really did all day was design my Micro-Blaster. That's what I ended up calling Star Jumper's security system. Even when my schoolbooks were open and I was staring at the teacher, I was actually doing calculations in my head. I could see her mouth moving, but half the time I didn't have a clue what she was talking about.

The basic design was a breeze. Power in. Power out. Zap! It was all a matter of hyper-induction. You'd have to understand quantum mechanics to know what I was really up to. So unless you're a mathematician of the highest rank, I won't bore you with the details.

All you need to know is that by lunchtime I had mastered the math necessary to make a medium-sized mountain range disappear. No small achievement — even for a genius of my caliber.

I'm sure the math alone is worth a Nobel Prize.

But designing my security system to conform to Mom's rule — that's what took real brains. You see, my mom doesn't like guns. She especially hates how they're made to seem cool in the movies and on TV. She always says "With all the senseless wars in the world today, you'd think writers could come up with stories for kids that don't involve violence." Mom feels so strongly about this that she made me promise never to play with guns or anything that could hurt anyone.

So how was I going to build a security system that really worked? It seemed like an impossible task. Right? I have to admit that I almost gave up at one point and broke my promise. But by the end of the day, true genius that I am, I came up with the perfect solution.

My Micro-Blaster won't actually *hurt* anything. Instead of destroying or killing aliens, it will just shrink them down to a size so small they become harmless! Brilliant, huh? Imagine an alien Tyrannosaurus rex. One minute it's bigger than a double-decker bus. Then ZAP! POOF! It's the size of a flea and you need a magnifying glass to see it.

Alien Dino-Flea

I put the final touches on my Micro-Blaster design halfway through study hall. The rest of the time I spent looking at the girl in the seat directly in front of me. It's stupid, I know, but I can't help myself. I guess every great genius has a weakness. Mine is Zoe Breen's long brown hair.

Zoe is one of the smartest girls at Whitman Elementary, and her hair is so shiny and soft looking that I can't stop staring at it. Sometimes I spend the whole study hall pretending to read. What I'm really doing is looking out the corner of my eye at Zoe Breen's hair. One time, when no one was looking, I even reached out and touched it! It was so smooth. Like silk.

Zoe Breen

This particular afternoon, Zoe ran her fingers through her hair, and one long strand drifted like a feather to the floor. I looked around. Everyone else was busy studying.

I don't know why but I just *had* to have it. I reached down and scooped it up. It was in my hand when Zoe suddenly turned around and saw what I was doing. I was never so embarrassed in my whole life. I know I must have blushed because my face felt red hot.

"I think this belongs to you," I said, trying my best to act cool.

"That's okay," she replied. "You can have it."

I've been watching Zoe Breen since the beginning of the school year. But this was the first time we actually talked face-to-face, person-to-person. And she was smiling at me!

It felt like there was no one else in the room. No one else in the school. No one else in the entire world! We were *all* alone and someone had just thrown a lever, jerking time to a screeching halt. There I was, probably the smartest person in the civilized world, and suddenly my tongue was made of granite. I just sat there like a dummy, unable to utter a single word.

Finally Zoe broke the spell.

"What's that?" she asked, looking at my page of calculations.

"Oh nothing," I replied, finding my voice again. "Just a little math work for extra credit."

"Hmmmm …" she said. "It looks kind of *advanced*."

I loved the way she said *"advanced,"* like it was her way of letting me know she understood how really smart and totally special I am.

Then the bell rang and it was all over.

"Got to go," she said.

In a few minutes I was the only one left in study hall, still sitting there holding a single strand of brown hair.

When no one was looking, I carefully wrapped it in a piece of notebook paper and decided to take it with me when I leave Planet Earth.

CHAPTER 8

The Micro-Blaster

After school I endured yet another bus ride home with Jonathan. Oh, brother! He was *still* talking about *Thursday Night Wrestling*. This time I didn't even try to shut him up. I just stared out the window thinking about Zoe Breen and my Micro-Blaster.

As soon as I got home, I started my search for building materials. I found most of what I needed in the plastic bins under my bed.

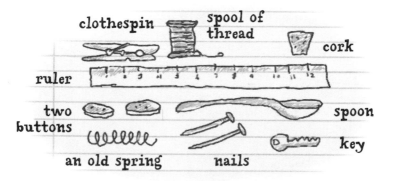

clothespin   spool of thread   cork

ruler

two buttons   spoon

an old spring   nails   key

I scored some more stuff from the attic. But I was still missing a few important items to make a deflector cone to focus an ion beam. I was totally stumped, until I remembered Dad's workshop in the garage. *That's where I'll find what I need!* I thought. What I didn't expect to find was my dad.

"Hi, Alex," he said, looking up from the board he was measuring.

Dad's been wanting to build new bookcases for the den since he learned how to read. At least, it seems that way. Every once in a while he actually cuts a few boards and hammers a few nails. But he works such long hours at the office that he never seems to get anywhere.

"You're home from work early," I said.

"Uh-huh." He made a mark on the board with his pencil. "My oldest patient fired me today."

"Gee … Sorry, Dad," I said.

"Oh no. It's not like that," he replied. "Not at all. In fact, I'm celebrating. You see, this patient came to me to help him overcome his fear of flying. And last week he got his pilot's license."

"Oh, that's great," I said, and to myself I thought, *Dad's a real miracle worker when it comes to solving other people's problems. Too bad he can't solve my problem: Jonathan.*

Dad smiled and switched on his radial arm saw.

"Can you hold the other end of this board for me?" he asked.

"Sure," said Jonathan, popping out of nowhere.

How the little insect got there I don't know. I should have expected it. He's always butting in between me and Dad. The next thing I knew, the garage was screaming with the sound of Dad's saw and Jonathan was holding that stupid board.

That was fine with me because just then I

spotted a piece of aluminum in Dad's trash barrel that was the perfect shape and size for my deflector cone.

"Can I have this?" I asked.

My dad had his ear protectors on.

"What?" he screamed above the whine of the saw.

"This!" I held up the piece of aluminum and shouted. "Can I have it?"

"Sure!" he shouted back. "You can have anything you want from that barrel. There's nothing in there but junk."

Junk? Dad may have thought so, but I found everything I needed to complete my security system in that barrel.

I went back to my room and got to work. In a mere twenty minutes, my Micro-Blaster was ready to test. Yet another record of engineering excellence and speed!

The Micro-Blaster looked more like something you'd toss a salad with than a high-tech security device.

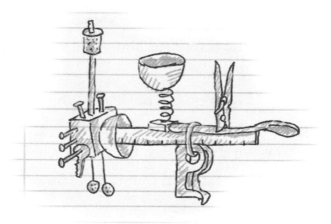

The Micro-Blaster

But I didn't care what it looked like. It just had to do the job. And it had to be handy in case of an emergency. That meant making a holster for it.

First I tried customizing one of Dad's old toy six-shooter sets that I found in the attic. That looked cool but the Blaster kept falling out. So I started scrounging around for other materials. I ended up making a holster from a bent coat hanger, a few pieces of cardboard and lots of duct tape. Voilà! In ten minutes it was done.

I couldn't wait to try out my latest invention. I thought of taking it down the street and aiming it at a few cars and trucks. If I zapped them to the size of toys, I could take them with me when I go and give them away to aliens as peace offerings.

Just then Mom called me from the kitchen. I could tell from the sound of her voice that she was angry, so I took my time going down the stairs. She was angry all right.

"You're behind on your chores, *dear*." The way she said *"dear"* sounded sweet, but I knew her better than that. She was looking past me at the kitchen trash bin, so I knew right away what chore she was talking about — taking out the garbage. It was part of a new arrangement "to teach me some responsibility." Jonathan, of course, doesn't have any chores because Mom and Dad think he's too young. I guess his only responsibility is to make me miserable.

"No problem, Mom," I said and took the white plastic garbage bag out of the bin and carried it to the backyard.

The trashcans were behind the tool shed. But I didn't see any reason to drag the bag all the way back there. I just set it on the lawn and stepped back a few feet. Then I unholstered my Micro-Blaster. I set the power level on low, pointed and pulled the trigger. For a second or two, nothing seemed to happen. *Maybe there's something wrong with my design,* I thought. *Maybe it was that bent nail I used in the tri-fibrillator. A thumbtack might have worked better.*

But the delay was just the time the device needed to build up a charge. Suddenly I felt a warm jolt and the stock of the Blaster buzzed in my hand. It was similar to the vibration of an electric toothbrush. Then there was a burst of light like a camera flash going off.

It wasn't anything dramatic like you'd see at the movies. But when I looked up, the trash bag had disappeared! Of course, it just *seemed* to disappear. It was actually still there — only now it was the size of a grain of rice. Poof! Lost in the grass somewhere.

The Micro-Blaster was a stunning success. Another major invention to add to my list of astounding achievements!

"Holy Cow!" I heard a cry, and Jonathan jumped out from behind the juniper bushes. His mouth was wide open, and his eyes looked as big as Frisbees. "That was *way* cool!"

I could see why he was impressed. Heck! What Jonathan just witnessed would impress the pants off the best scientist at Harvard or MIT. Even all the government scientists who work on top-secret stuff would drool all over their lab coats to get their hands on my Micro-Blaster.

"Yeah, it was cool all right," I said. "But you better not tell anyone about it! Especially Mom or Dad."

I was about to put the Blaster in its holster when Jonathan came toward me.

"Don't worry. I won't tell," he said. "Just let me hold it."

The urge to point the Blaster at him was irresistible. *Why should I be the one to leave this planet?* I thought. *All I have to do is shrink Jonathan to the size of a small bug, and my problems are over!* It was tempting. But I knew it wouldn't work. Somehow, Mom and Dad would find out, and I'd only have to bring him back.

"No way!" I said. "It's too dangerous for a little kid."

Jonathan was holding out his hand.

"I won't pull the trigger," he promised. "Really I won't."

"Why don't you go help Dad cut another board?"

"That's no fun. Just let me touch it. Show me how it works."

"No," I said. "Get out of here before I —"

I don't recall if Jonathan lunged first and bumped into me or if I just accidentally pulled the trigger.

All I remember was the flash and the look of total shock on Jonathan's face the instant before he disappeared.

CHAPTER 9

Godzilla Ant

I have to confess I considered just walking away. *Jonathan's gone. Gone forever. Hallelujah! My problems are over!* Instead of leaving for another planet, I pictured myself fabulously rich and famous, living happily ever after with Zoe Breen by my side.

But I knew I was dreaming. Jonathan hadn't really disappeared. I saw something fall into the grass. It had to be him. *Jonathan may be as small as a bug right now,* I thought, *but he won't survive for long down there in the grass living like one.* I just *had* to bring him back.

If only I could reverse the ion flow!

I knew it was theoretically possible. But would my Blaster actually work in reverse? All I had to do was switch the red and blue wires to find out. Boy, was I scared! All of a sudden I was so clumsy I reminded myself of Jonathan trying to put a worm on a hook. My fingers felt like sausages.

"Don't go anywhere, Jonathan!" I hollered into the grass. "Stay right where you are."

I thought I heard him call back but I couldn't be sure. It was just a high-pitched squeak, like an insect sound.

"What?" I called.

I heard the sound again. It went on for a long time, but I couldn't make out a single word.

Finally I switched the wires and pointed the Blaster to the spot where I thought Jonathan had landed.

I pulled the trigger and the device revved up again.

"This better work," I said to myself. "If it doesn't I'm sunk! No one will ever believe I didn't do this on purpose."

There was a bright pink flash. It was so bright it lit up the whole backyard and blinded me for a few seconds.

When the pink glare cleared from my eyes, I realized that something terrible had gone wrong. Standing in front of me was a huge black ant. When I say huge, I mean HUGE! Right away I knew what had happened. My aim was off. Instead of expanding Jonathan to his normal size, the ion beam had struck an ant. And now that ant was as big as a refrigerator!

I needed to reverse the wires again and shrink Godzilla Ant back to normal. But I was so totally *freaked*. My fingers felt like *frozen* sausages!

The ant looked disoriented. It touched the grass with its feelers and looked all around as if trying to figure out what had happened. Then I guess its instinct to gather food took over and I suddenly looked appetizing. It came at me with its pincers clicking like lobster claws.

Godzilla Ant

I turned and ran for shelter. The nearest place to hide was the tool shed. I ran inside, slammed the door and locked it. *Calm down,* I told myself. *As long as you stay in this shed you're safe.*

While I fumbled with the wires in my Micro-Blaster, the ant came around to the side window. As I pushed the red wire in place and screwed it down with my thumbnail, I heard a crashing sound. Pieces of shattered glass rained down all around me.

The ant's head was poking through the window.

"Yikes!" I cried and jumped back to avoid its snapping pincers.

In all the confusion, I dropped the Blaster into Mom's watering can. Kerplunk!

"Holy Copernicus! Please don't let the tri-fibrillator short-circuit!" I prayed out loud. Then I fished out the Blaster and dried it off with an old rag.

Meanwhile the tool shed was starting to rock back and forth. I looked down and realized it had no floor. Suddenly a tiny factoid popped into my brain: *Ants can lift twenty times their own body weight!*

One side of the shed rocked up off the ground. The ant was lifting it with one claw and the other was coming straight for me. My shelter had become a trap and I had nowhere to go!

I felt so dumb. A true genius outwitted by an ant! How could that be? I dodged the claw and fit

the blue wire in place. Then I pointed the Blaster
at the ant and pulled the trigger.

The shed fell to the ground.

When I opened the door, the ant was nowhere
to be seen. *Probably back in the grass looking for
something else to eat,* I thought. *Whew! That was a
close one!*

I ran to the spot where I had left Jonathan. But
I wasn't sure where it was anymore. I got down on

my knees, hoping I wasn't crushing him, and parted the grass blades with my fingers.

"Jonathan! Where are you?" I called.

Once again I heard that squeaking sound. Then I saw something move. It looked like a little blue pebble wearing a baseball cap. Somehow, Jonathan had climbed up out of the grass onto a dandelion leaf. The little blue pebble was jumping up and down and waving its tiny arms.

"Hold on, Jonathan," I yelled. "Just hold on!"

This time, after reversing the ion flow, I pointed the Blaster *precisely* at my target.

BAM! There was another brilliant pink flash.

When my sight returned to normal, Jonathan was standing before me. He looked a tiny bit taller but not so much that anyone would notice.

"I'm telling!" he cried and started running toward the house.

"Wait!" I ran after him. "I'll let you touch it. Really, I will."

Jonathan stopped and looked at me, staring long and hard. His eyes were bloodshot. His cheeks were wet from crying. I had never seen him look so scared.

"I almost got run over by a slimy slug!" he whimpered between short breaths.

"It was an accident," I said and held the Blaster out to him. "Here, I'll show you how it works."

"No!" he drew back. "I'm going to tell Mom and Dad. That thing's no good!"

Not just Mom. Mom *and* Dad. When he

threatened that, I knew he was serious. I had really terrified him and he meant to get my Micro-Blaster taken away from me.

"Look, you don't have to worry about me using *this* ever again," I said.

"Why?" he asked.

"Because I'm leaving."

My words hit him like a punch in the belly, the kind that takes your breath away.

I should have kept my mouth shut. But once I got started I couldn't stop.

"I'm going to another planet. That's why I built the spaceship. And that's why you don't have to worry about this Blaster, because when I leave I'm taking it with me."

"Really?"

"Really," I answered.

"Can I come with you?"

"No," I said. "Don't you get it? *You're* the reason I'm leaving."

Jonathan looked like someone had punched him in the belly again, only harder this time.

"Oh," was all he said.

"That's why you don't have to worry about me blasting you anymore," I told him.

Suddenly Jonathan's eyes looked cold and mean.

"Well, you're not going to like it there," he stammered. "You're not going to like it one bit!"

"Oh yeah?" I asked. "Why's that?"

"Because the only planet you'd like is a planet where everyone on it is exactly like you," he replied. "And that doesn't exist!"

CHAPTER 10

The Duplicator

Jonathan didn't know it, but he had just given me a *fantastic* idea: Duplication!

Deep down, I was feeling a little nervous about going to a strange planet. The inhabitants might not be warlike (they might be as peaceful as toadstools — heck, they might even *be* toadstools!), but what if I didn't like *them*? What if they were boring? Or so smart I couldn't understand what they were talking about?

Planet Toadstool

Or what if I found a planet that I liked — nice mountains, green trees, good volcanoes — but *no* people? After a while, even I, the great me, might get a little lonely. But not if I had other me's to talk to.

The solution was obvious: *duplicate* myself! What I needed was a machine that could instantly create an actual duplication of a human being. *Brilliant.* Don't you agree? Just think about it. Even if I landed on a planet with some interesting people, I'd still want a dozen or so me's around. I mean, who wouldn't?

I have to admit, if Jonathan hadn't said what he did, I never would have come up with the idea of duplication.

But having an idea was one thing. Actually designing and building a Duplicator was another.

This was my toughest challenge yet. After dinner I went to my room and locked the door. Then I climbed into bed, pulled the covers over my head and just lay there trying to come up with a brilliant idea. But I wasn't getting anywhere. In fact, I fell asleep without a single breakthrough.

That night, however, I had a dream. Next to my bed I have a globe of Planet Earth. I've had it since I was a little kid, younger than Jonathan. In my dream, my bedroom is crowded with globes. There are five of them on my desk. Ten in my closet. And my floor is wall-to-wall globes, all of them spinning! I hear the phone ring and jump out of bed to answer it. But all of a sudden I fall into a giant space, like a football stadium, filled from top to bottom with nothing but globes.

When I woke up, it hit me — parallel universes! I don't have to build a machine that actually makes new me's. An endless number of me's, exact copies of myself, already exist in parallel universes. All I have to do is make a machine to suck them out of their world and into mine!

The idea was solid. But could I make the math work? I sharpened some pencils, opened my special notebooks and dug in. Once again I amazed myself. In mere minutes I solved problems teams of professors armed with rooms of supercomputers wouldn't begin to understand for decades.

The design work went quickly, too. I decided to build a large model first. Work out the glitches. Then build one small enough to fit inside Star Jumper. It was a smart plan, but it meant I was going to need more cardboard boxes.

Luckily, it was Saturday, Mom's regular shopping day. So I asked if I could go along.

"Why this interest in shopping lately?" she wanted to know.

"I need some more boxes —" I began.

"For my castle!" cried Jonathan.

"If you don't mind, I think I'd rather pick up the boxes for you, Alex," said Mom. "Jonathan already asked to come along, and I'm not up to dealing with both of you fighting in the store."

"That's okay," I said. "I'd rather not be anywhere *he* is anyway."

"Oh yeah! Me neither!" said Jonathan, poking his head out from behind Mom's butt and making that squinty-eyed imp face of his.

"This is exactly what I mean!" said Mom with a sigh.

I was glad when they finally got in the van and drove away. At last, some peace and quiet.

I quickly gathered the spare parts and additional pieces I would need when the cardboard arrived. Then for a reward I went into the kitchen and made myself a peanut butter and grape jelly sandwich.

As I ate my sandwich, I looked out the kitchen window and watched a chickadee and a nuthatch fighting over birdseed at the feeder. What birdbrains! If only they got along and took turns, they'd each get a lot more to eat. I made a mental note to look into the problem and see what I could invent for them someday. Then I remembered that I wasn't going to be around here much longer, and that made me feel kind of sad.

To cheer myself up, I took my snack into the living room and turned on some cartoons. The old ones are my favorites. As I sat there watching, I couldn't help but wonder if somewhere out there in the galaxy I'd find a planet with cartoons as good as *Daffy Duck* and *Bugs Bunny*.

Finally Mom pulled in and beeped her horn to let me know she needed help carrying in the bags.

When I got out to the driveway, she was bent over the back seat trying her best to wake up Jonathan.

"Come on, sweetie!" she said as she unbuckled his seatbelt. "Wake up. We're home now."

If it were up to me, I'd leave "sweetie" in the car for the rest of the day.

Jonathan was mumbling, "No. No! Slimy slugs! Get away from me!"

"Can you make out what he's saying, Alex?" asked Mom. "He's been mumbling in his sleep all the way home."

"Beats me," I replied and checked out the boxes. She got all the right sizes and a few extras. I was thrilled.

"Thanks, Mom," I said. "These are great."

By the time my mom and I carried in the groceries, Jonathan was wide-awake and begging to help put things away.

Of course, he wasn't much help. "The ice cream doesn't go in the cupboard, Flea brain!" I said. "It goes in the freezer."

"But it's easier to reach down here!" Jonathan insisted.

When the groceries were put away, I stacked the boxes one inside the other and started up to my room.

"Oh, Alex?" My mom stopped me on the stairs. "I was wondering if you could do me a favor."

I tried not to roll my eyeballs because I know it annoys her. But I couldn't help it.

"What?" I said and put down my boxes.

"Could you be a good big brother and watch Jonathan while I catch up on my e-mail?" she asked. I hate it when she does that "good big brother" thing. "It's so hard to concentrate when he's around and —"

"You can say that again," I said.

"Please," said Mom, giving me her best sad-eyed puppy look. "I *did* get those boxes for you —"

"Okay, okay," I gave in. "Where is the little brat?"

"Right here," said a voice directly behind me. (I swear that kid is half leprechaun.) "And I'm not a little brat."

Jonathan had taken one of my boxes and put it over his head, so only his feet were visible.

"Okay, you're not a little brat. You're a big brat. A *gigantic* brat. Is that better?"

"Much better," said Jonathan and we went upstairs.

CHAPTER 11

Two of Me

"So what are these new boxes for?" asked Jonathan. "You're going to build me a castle before you leave, right?"

"Not so loud," I said and shut my bedroom door.

I took out my knife and tape and plastic bins and got to work.

"Well?" asked Jonathan.

"Well what?" I replied.

"Are you going to build me a castle or not?"

"What do you think?" I said.

Jonathan was quiet for a while. He just stood there and watched me. Then he asked, "Can I have one of those boxes?"

I had a box or two to spare. I also saw an opportunity.

"That all depends," I said. "Are you going to be good?"

Jonathan put on his angel face.

"Sure, I'll be really good."

"I don't believe you."

His normal squinty-eyed devil look returned.

"Well, I want one anyway!" he insisted.

"Here, take this one," I said. "But the first time you bother me, I'm taking it back. Go over there as far away from me as possible and don't talk unless I talk to you first. Understand?"

I pointed to the far corner of my room.

Jonathan took the box, sighed and marched into the corner.

"What are you going to do with your boxes?" he asked.

"I'm going to build a device," I said.

"What kind of device?"

"I don't know yet," I lied.

"Good," said Jonathan. "Because that's what

I'm going to do, too. And I'm not telling you what it is either. So there!"

I had lots of tools, gadgets and other odds and ends from my bins and the bottom drawer of my desk. I had a hammer, a saw, two kinds of screwdrivers, wheels, dials, knobs, springs, Popsicle sticks, pipe cleaners … Everything you need to invent anything in the world.

All Jonathan had to work with was a big black crayon and the little pieces of junk he carried around in his pockets.

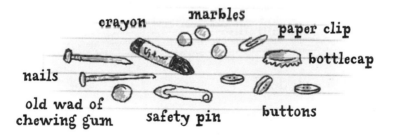

marbles
crayon
paper clip
bottlecap
nails
old wad of
chewing gum
safety pin
buttons

In a way he reminded me of myself — that's just how I was when I was his age and started building stuff.

I set to work on my Duplicator, taping and adding dials, indicator knobs and switches. While I worked I noticed Jonathan out of the corner of my eye. First he drew a strange geometric pattern on his box. Then he poked holes in the pattern and inserted odd bits of wire, marbles and bottle caps into them. Thank heaven he was quiet for a change.

My own work went amazingly fast. In no time at all, I had a large-scale Duplicator ready to test.

"There. I'm done," I announced.

"Me too," said Jonathan.

"That doesn't look like much," I said. "What does it do?"

"It's a secret," he replied. "What does yours do?"

I thought of not telling him. That's always been my policy. But today I felt generous. After all, Jonathan was the source of my original inspiration.

"I call it a Duplicator," I said.

The Duplicator

"What's it duplicate?"

"Anything that goes in it," I answered. "Even people."

"That's impossible," said Jonathan.

"Not if it pulls your duplicate from a parallel universe," I explained.

Jonathan nodded his head as if he understood what I was talking about.

"Show me," he said.

I figured I had to test it out anyway. So why not turn my test into a demonstration?

"Okay," I said. I pushed the power button and set the quantity dial to 1. The device started up right away but shook a little and made a low hum. That didn't seem right. Any motion or sound in the unit was an indication of misalignment and was bound to cause distortion. So I got out my screwdriver and made a few adjustments until it was perfectly still and quiet. Then I stepped inside.

"Now what?" asked Jonathan.

"Just a …" I flipped the copy switch and suddenly two of me stepped out of the Duplicator "… second," we both said.

It was a very odd sensation being *two* instead of *one. This is going to take some getting used to,* I thought. But already I could tell I was going to like it.

Jonathan looked back and forth at the two me's as if he were trying to decide which one was real.

ME   ME

"I'm the real Alex," said both of us.

"No you're not!" I said to the duplicate.

I thought Jonathan would be impressed. But he wasn't.

"Want to see what I made?" he asked.

Just then the phone rang.

"Alex, telephone!" Mom shouted from downstairs.

"Be right there," said both of me.

"No, you stay here and keep an eye on Jonathan," I said to my duplicate.

"Okay, but don't be long," replied the duplicate. He looked at Jonathan suspiciously. "I don't trust that kid. Not one bit."

I ran downstairs and picked up the phone.

"Hi, Alex," said a soft voice. "This is Zoe. I hope you don't mind that I called. I got your number from the phone book."

CHAPTER 12

The Disappearing Device

I was kind of shocked — a girl calling me at home? That had never happened before.

"Uh … Hi," I replied. I thought my voice sounded a little shaky — like I was scared or something.

"I forgot our math assignment," said Zoe. "Do you remember what it was?"

Zoe *always* writes down math assignments in her little blue assignment book. I watch her do it every day. So I knew right away she had something else on her mind. In fact I was pretty sure she was just using homework as an excuse to call me up. I took a deep breath and counted to three before I spoke.

"There is no math homework, remember?" I said.

There was a long silence.

I really liked the idea that Zoe had called me up. But I also couldn't stop thinking about what might be going on in my bedroom.

Suddenly Zoe said something totally unexpected.

"Umm … you wouldn't be interested in going to a movie with me this afternoon, would you? The Mummy's Purse … er … I mean *The Mummy's Curse* is playing."

She sure sounded nervous. I would be too if I were the one doing the asking. Actually, I'd thought about going to a movie with Zoe lots of times. But I'd never got up the nerve to ask.

"What … ah … er …" I didn't know what to say. I'd heard that *The Mummy's Curse* had a terrific story with lots of cool special effects. In the end the mummy eats itself! I really wanted to see it. And

Zoe Breen was just the person I wanted to see it with. Heck, I'd even watch *Thursday Night Wrestling* with Zoe. But going to a movie with a girl? I wasn't ready for this. What if someone from school saw us? They'd say I have a girlfriend. I didn't think I could stand all the teasing.

"Yeah, well, um …" I was fishing around for what to say when I heard some strange noises coming from my room. "Actually, I saw *The Mummy's Curse*. It was great," I lied. "Oops, my mom is calling me. Got to go now! Bye!" I lied again and hung up.

You idiot! I thought as I flew up the stairs to my room. *That was your last chance on Earth to go to the movies with Zoe Breen and you blew it! Are you a loser or what?*

As soon as I opened my bedroom door, I forgot all about Zoe and *The Mummy's Curse*. I had a curse of my own to deal with: curse of the rotten little brother. Standing before me, filling up my entire bedroom — sitting on the floor, on my chairs, on my bed and at my desk — were dozens of Jonathans! My brother, curse his evil little soul, had somehow disposed of the other me and duplicated himself about fifty times!

"Hi!" I was greeted by a chorus of high-pitched whiny voices.

"Where's the other me?" I cried.

"Oh, we made him disappear," said six or seven Jonathans as they pointed to the cardboard device on my desk.

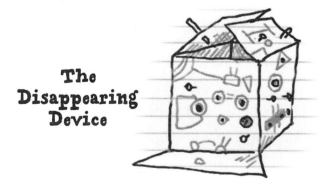

The Disappearing Device

"You what?" I said.

"We disappeared him," said another bunch of Jonathans. "That's what we built. A Disappearing Device."

Jonathan's device looked more like an art project than a scientific invention. But who was I to be fussy about appearances? I have to admit I felt a twinge of brotherly pride. *He must have got some of my genius genes after all,* I thought. No matter what it looked like, Jonathan's invention was brilliant!

Meanwhile, the room was crawling with Jonathans. Five or six Jonathans were looking through my stamp collection. A few were going through my drawers, trying on clothes that didn't fit. Just as many more were staging mock air battles with my jet plane models. "Eeeeerrrrrooow! Bam! Bam! Bam! Gotcha!"

A bunch of Jonathans were jumping on my bed. "Now we can do whatever we want to!" they chanted as they bounced up and down.

"Okay." I put my hands on my hips. "Who's the real Jonathan here?"

Suddenly the room became quiet. I looked from face to face. They all stared back at me with big-eyed innocent looks.

Then all fifty or so Jonathans responded, *"I am!"*

I felt like bolting from the room, locking the door and calling the police. Then I reminded myself, *It's just your little brother. You can handle him. Right?*

I walked up to one of the Jonathans and grabbed him by the arm. Suddenly all the other Jonathans gave me a "don't you dare" look and pressed forward.

I stopped and looked around. It was the worst nightmare imaginable: I was surrounded by an army of rotten little brothers, and there was nothing I could do about it. Suddenly it felt like *I* was the little brother. I released the Jonathan I was holding and straightened out the wrinkles on his shirt.

Immediately a big grin lit up all the Jonathans' faces. They knew they had me. I was at their mercy and they *liked* it. They liked it a lot!

Then I had an idea.

"You know, you're very clever," I said and edged closer to the Disappearing Device.

Some of the Jonathans saw what I had in mind. Before I could get near, they closed ranks and made a wall of Jonathans around the device. I had hoped to use it to get rid of the mob of little brothers. Now I had to think really fast. I made a dash to my Duplicator. I turned up the quantity dial to 10, jumped inside and flipped the copy switch.

Raaam zat!

It worked like a charm. The Duplicator made not just one additional Alex, but ten! Now there were eleven of me in the room. Before any of the Jonathans could retaliate, I flipped the copy switch again. Now there were twenty-one of me! Enough to overpower the Jonathans protecting the Disappearing Device and take it away from them. Or so I hoped.

"Get them!" cried Jonathans all around me.

As they leaped into action, my bedroom burst into a churning battle of wrestling brothers. When one of the Jonathans threw some pillows into the Duplicator, the battle quickly turned into a gigantic pillow fight. Feathers were flying everywhere! In no time at all, it looked like a snow blizzard had hit my room.

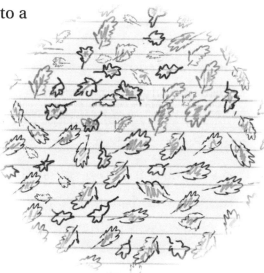

There were more Jonathans than Alexes but we were bigger and stronger. The Jonathans had captured my Duplicator and were making more copies of themselves. But I had already turned the quantity dial back to 1 and removed the dial. So now all they could make was one Jonathan at a time.

Then our side got control of the Disappearing Device.

"Cover him!" called one of the other me's in the room. I soon found myself surrounded by an army of bodyguards.

For every Jonathan the other side duplicated, I made three or four disappear. The first ten or so were easy to zap because the room was jumping with Jonathans. I hardly had to aim. All I had to do was point, shoot and — POOF! They were gone!

But I had to be careful. Once I missed, and a

whole stack of books on my floor disappeared. Again and again, groups of five or six Jonathans rushed me for the Disappearing Device.

"That's ours," they cried. "Give it back!"

Luckily, my bodyguards protected me, and the enemy never got close.

After a while, the crowd of Jonathans thinned out and it was a little harder zapping my targets. When I got down to the last batch of Jonathans, they started hiding and begging for mercy. Some slid under my bed. Others ran to the closet. I locked my door and dropped the key into my pocket so none could escape.

"No! Don't zap me," they all pleaded at the last moment. "I'm the real Jonathan! You don't want to disappear your own little brother. Do you?"

"You bet I do!" I said and zapped them just the same. As far as I was concerned, they were all *exact* duplicates. So there was no such thing as the *real* Jonathan.

"That's for talking all the time!" I cried. POOF! "And that's for the way you eat!" POOF! "And that's for boiling my tropical fish!" POOF! "And that's for the Honey Puffs!" POOF!

"Hey, wait a minute," cried a few Jonathans. "We never boiled your fish!"

"Maybe not," I hollered. "But you were glad when they died! Weren't you?" POOF! POOF! POOF!

Finally, I got down to one last little brother. I backed him into a corner and pushed the Disappearing Device in his face.

"You did kill my fish, didn't you?" I said. "Tell the truth!"

"Yeah, I did," he confessed in a whimper. A single tear streamed down his left cheek and fell into the corner of his mouth. "But I didn't mean to. And I wasn't glad when they died. I just wanted to see what would happen when I turned up the heat. I wanted to see if they would swim faster."

My poor little fish! I thought. *At least they died in the quest for scientific truth.* I could hardly fault Jonathan for that.

Just then Mom started pounding on the door.

"What's going on in there?" she cried and tried the doorknob. "Open this door at once!"

"What are we going to do?" said one of my duplicates.

"We?" I replied.

His expression turned sour. "You have to get rid of us. Don't you?"

"That's right," I said and started zapping all the other Alexes in the room. Luckily, they all knew it had to be done and went willingly.

When there were five or six left, Jonathan asked, "Can I finish off the rest?"

I don't know why but I said "Okay" and handed him the Disappearing Device. "But you have to give it back when you're done. No funny business!"

"No funny business," he replied.

POOF! POOF! POOF!

When there was just me and Jonathan left, I fished the key out of my pocket and unlocked the door.

Mom looked into the room and didn't say a word. But I could see her lips move as she counted to ten.

"I want you to know I'm feeling a lot of anger right now," she began calmly, but pretty soon she was screaming. "THIS PLACE LOOKS LIKE IT GOT HIT BY A BOMB! WHAT IS WRONG WITH YOU TWO?"

"I was doing you a favor, Mom," I said. "Remember?"

She looked around the room. "You call this a favor? What were you two fighting about this time?"

"Oh, we weren't fighting," I said and carefully put the Disappearing Device on my top shelf, just out of Jonathan's reach. "We were playing."

Mom seemed to like that answer. So did Jonathan.

"Yeah, we were just playing," he said with a big grin.

CHAPTER 13

My Most Brilliant Creation

"Well, I'm glad to hear that you two were having fun," said Mom. "But this room is still a mess. I want it cleaned up right now!"

She was right about the mess. Three inches of feathers covered the floor. My desk was tipped over. A chair was on top of my bed. There were blankets and pillowcases, lampshades and clothes, and airplane models and stuff from my plastic bins all over the place.

And my spaceship! My precious Star Jumper was totally destroyed — scattered around the room like leaves on the lawn.

I was crushed. But I saw no point in crying like a baby or throwing a temper tantrum. *After all*, I told myself, *I still have all my sketches and notes. Whatever a true genius does once he can do again!*

Besides, at that moment I was thinking about something else entirely.

"Could we clean up later?" I asked my mom.

"Later?" She frowned.

"Yeah, I was thinking of taking Jonathan to a matinee. *The Mummy's Curse* is playing down at the Fox."

Both Mom and Jonathan stared at me as if I had just turned into a hot dog or something.

I could almost hear Mom thinking: *Am I hallucinating or did Alex just volunteer to do something nice for his little brother?*

"Sure, that sounds great," she said, unable to disguise a note of suspicion in her voice. Maybe she thought I was planning to take him to a movie and never bring him home again. "But both of you have to clean up this mess as soon as you get back. Do you hear that, Jonathan? You have to help, too."

"That's okay with me," said the stinker.

Jonathan didn't care what he had to do. He was in little brother heaven. I was taking him to a movie. And nobody had twisted my arm to do it! Without being told, he immediately ran to the bathroom, washed his face and put on a clean shirt.

All the way to the Fox, Jonathan's feet hardly seemed to touch the ground. But that didn't stop him from being obnoxious. As soon as we got our tickets, he insisted that I buy him popcorn.

"A movie without popcorn is like a doughnut without a hole," he said, quoting our dad.

Normally I would want popcorn, too, but not today. Today I definitely had something else on my mind.

"Just chew on your nails or suck your thumb if you get hungry," I said.

The coming attractions were ending as we stepped into the dark theater.

I scanned the audience to find Zoe and spotted her right away. She was sitting just where I like to sit — in the exact middle of the front row. I sat down right next to her.

I had my little brother along. So no one could accuse me of going to a movie with a girl. I was *not* on a date. I could sit anywhere I wanted. Even next to Zoe Breen with her long brown hair and pretty eyes. (Did I mention her eyes? Well, they're soft and deep and blue.) And no one could tease me about it at school on Monday.

I had to smile at my own genius. I had done the impossible! My greatest achievement ever. My pièce de résistance! I had figured out a good use for my little brother. I'd already created many fantastic inventions that will make me world famous someday. And I'm sure there will be many more to come. But so far, this was my most brilliant creation of all!

My New Mission

In case you think I've gone completely soft in the head and canceled my plans to find a new home somewhere else in the universe, you're wrong. I'm just delaying my trip for a while. That's all.

My little brother is still the biggest pain in the butt this side of Alpha Centauri. I do *not* intend to spend the rest of my precious youth living on the same planet with him.

I'm just hoping Zoe will want to come along. If she does I'm going to double the size of Star Jumper 2 and take her with me. That's my new mission. I haven't worked out the details yet, but you know me. Bim! Bam! Once I get going, it won't take long.

And now that I know that my little brother, rotten brat that he is, is also a great inventor like myself, I might let him work on a few refinements. For example, I want to outfit Star Jumper 2 with an Asteroid Repeller and an Anti-gravity Device for walking on really big planets. Perhaps I'll let him help with those.

And maybe in return, if he doesn't bug me too much, I'll build him one small castle.

But I'll never be his horse!